Gabriel Anthony Lopez

AZIMUTHAL

To order additional copies of this book, contact:
Xlibris
844-714-8691
www.Xlibris.com
Orders@Xlibris.com

ISBN:	Softcover	978-1-6641-7510-5
Hardcover	978-1-6641-7511-2
EBook	978-1-6641-7509-9

Library of Congress Control Number: 2021909957

Print information available on the last page.

Rev. date: 05/17/2021

This book is dedicated to my loving and caring mother.

She was one of the world's best. I will always remember those times she was at my swim team meets, Boy Scouts, and academic events. I will remember her wittiness and attentiveness for the events to the greater outside world. As a mom, she was one of God's best. She put me through the best schooling she could think of, given where she was from and not thinking how much money it costs, and she always wished the world for me.

I

Geno looked out above Earth Station as it sped path Earth. Earth looked like it always had, minus some cyclonic activity in the Pacific Ocean. His father Krev just came in from a monitoring station and went into his bedroom. It was the year 2350, and Geno knew somehow his father was important to this mission about Earth. Geno quickly called Lunar Base where Ignacio was staying for the time.

"Hey," he said, "everything good at Lunar Base?"

"Yes," said Ignacio. "Lunar Base is checking in A-OK."

"How are things besides A-OK?" asked Geno.

"Well, the food started to dwindle a little while ago," answered Ignacio.

Geno put on his gravity boots since the antigravity generators started to deplete on Earth Station. He made his way cautiously down a long hallway to the food dispenser. Geno kept wondering about his father Krev and what the Planetary Defense for Geology and Geography was saying to him.

There had not been any seismic activity on Earth for quite some time, and they kept doing missions to the planet, and so did Lunar Base. Geno was only twenty-three years old Earth time, but lately, he could not sleep. He kept waking up as if he had forgotten something in the middle of the night Earth time. Geno looked up at a screen and touched it.

Ignacio popped up on it. He was shaving his face. Geno turned and put his half-eaten plate of food in a trash dispenser.

"So far, Lunar Base could be doing better," Ignacio said cynically. "I had to shave today."

"Ah, I see," said Geno.

Ignacio was from Mexico, but after the geologic cataclysm on Earth over a century ago, the country had allied with the rest of the Americas, especially where Geno was from, the United States of America. Geno looked down as he plodded his way through the mess hall and came across an old NASA decal and patch lying on the floor. That had changed also since the great cataclysm. The San Andreas Fault line had finally broken up, and California's major populations dwindled. The Yellowstone eruption had occurred. Thereafter, the planet stopped receiving seismic activity.

Ignacio was always the jokester. He probably paid someone to put them there to taunt Geno. Geno did not want to remember the great cataclysm, but he did know the ensuing planetary union, including Earth Station orbiting Earth and Lunar Base on the Moon.

"Well, despite our quiet conversation, I hope we're still friends, Geno," said Ignacio.

"Yes, we are," said Geno. "Ever since school and planetary induction that is."

"Have you been able to sleep?" asked Geno.

"No, my dreams have been wild, though, with the little sleep I've been getting," answered Ignacio.

"Really?" said Geno. "I've been waking as if I've been forgetting something, no dreaming at all."

Geno once read a book about dreams by Carl Jung. He wasn't sure if that was a good thing or a bad thing that Ignacio had been having wild dreams.

"What do you think of these dreams?" asked Geno.

"Well, at first, I'm relaxed, but then I'm afraid," answered Ignacio.

"Afraid of what?" asked Geno.

"The future, of course," answered Ignacio.

Ignacio clicked the screen to turn it off, bidding Geno a good day and good night until they contact each other again. Geno touched his gravity boots again. He made his way back to his bedroom. He wondered what his father Krev was doing. Once he walked in his bedroom, he took off his gravity boots again and began floating. He was tired after eating. And his father was still in his room; he heard him vaguely going through some papers and some computer pads. As Geno laid back on his bed, he could not help but wonder what Ignacio was saying about his dreaming. Maybe he would have some out-there dreams too.

II

The next day Krev woke Geno up. The Planetary Defense for Geology and Geography just had a meeting. The news was bad. The political situation on Earth collapsed because of increased seismic activity. Clandestine mining operations had been the culprit. Krev alerted Mars Base to see what they could do, if anything, to make Earth stable again. And there lay Kakuro. Kakuro was a friend of Geno's even during school and during planetary initiation into the Planetary Defense for Geology and Geography.

"C'mon, wake up," said Krev.

"Nope," said Geno. "I just had this dream. A dream you were at Mars before it was terraformed."

"Before it was terraformed!" said Krev. "You're seeing things. That happened almost a hundred years ago. C'mon, I have to show you something, Geno."

Geno's father had always been a mystery to him. His duties were a mystery to him. Geno at times felt like he was an old human word called "being sheltered." Krev never let him know what his real duties were.

"Where are we going?" asked Geno.

"You'll see!" answered Krev.

They grabbed their gravity boots; the gravity generators had not come back online. Krev seemed enthusiastic, but why? Geno wondered even more to himself. Was he finally going to tell him the secret to his duties at the Planetary Defense for Geology and Geography? Krev and Geno walked to a place called Stellar Cartography.

Krev scanned his hand over the console of Earth Base's Stellar Cartography. As soon as he did that, the room went dark, and Geno was covered with stars, and at the center was the solar system—our solar system. Geno tried to read his father's face but couldn't. It was a mixture of sadness and bluntness, like he was about to say something.

"Geno, have you ever felt you were meant for something—perhaps greater than yourself?" asked Krev.

"None," answered Geno.

"Well, today seismic activity on Earth started," said Krev.

Geno acknowledged this fact because Earth showed data signs. He touched the holographic image of Earth, and dots were connecting to all the recent seismic places on Earth had happened. "Too many," he murmured to himself.

Krev touched Earth Base twice, and Geno immediately found himself flying through the solar system and not on ion drive. The holographic demonstration suddenly stopped at Jupiter.

Geno knew Jupiter had a station simply called Jupiter Station, but he also knew what lay beyond that was dangerous. Why was his father showing this to him?

"Why Jupiter Station?" inquired Geno.

"Well," replied Krev, "seismic activity on Earth has started. And on Jupiter Station is the answer."

Geno knew from his planetary induction to the stations throughout the solar system that the stations had been collecting not just data and realized the secret to Earth's future was some kind of geologic healing process only found on the moons orbiting Jupiter.

"I think the Planetary Defense for Geology and Geography may send you to Jupiter Station," said Krev with a wink.

"You mean after all this time? Is everything all right, Father?" asked Geno.

Geno needed to tell someone this, perhaps Kakuro, one of his friends. But Kakuro already knew how his father wanted to tell Geno and ran away from the danger placed by his father. But like all humans, Geno had duties, even though he was only twenty-three years old. Geno winced physically at the suggestion. Krev would have none of this.

"Geno," said his father Krev, "you're on the first flight out to Mars Base then Jupiter Station."

Geno boarded the ion-powered spaceship. He had a computer pad in hand, and a holographic image of Kakuro popped up on the computer pad. Geno never liked sleep chambers in the ion ships. The journey would only last a month. There had been rumors of a true enemy out there, rumors of people dying in their hypersleep chambers. It was the rule of the Planetary Defense for Geology and Geography for every passenger to communicate via dreams in their sleep. Geno slowly walked out of an orbital from Earth Station. He had taken the elixir to slow down metabolic processes and assist the brain in the journey.

Geno became frightened as he neared the ship. Kakuro was phoning via the computer before the journey was beginning. Geno touched the computer pad.

"Ready for the long nap?" asked Kakuro.

"Well, maybe," answered Geno. "I'm going to go through the process of checking and rechecking the ship before the journey. I already took the elixir. I'm in one of the orbitals outside Earth Station."

"Okay, gotcha," said Kakuro.

Geno was nervous. As he walked through the orbital, he released his gravity boots and began to float to the docking point with the spaceship. He inserted his badge. Suddenly, the orbital did not let Geno in the ship. "Lockdown, initiated," said the computer.

Geno was wondering why the lockdown had been initiated. Geno began to panic. Outside was the glistening sphere of Earth, and as Geno peered through the glass of the orbital separating him from the cold outside of space, he saw Earth-bound ships being deployed from Earth Station. Earth Station seemed encumbered by recent seismic and geologic developments on Earth.

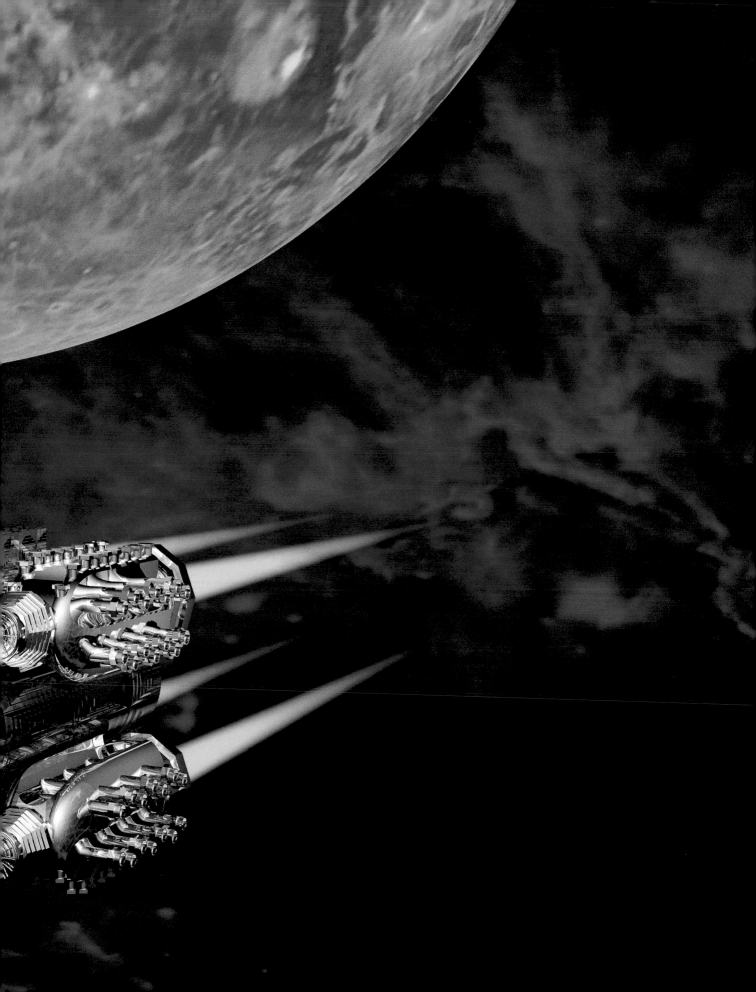

"Ships being deployed," said the computer.

Geno stopped panicking again and listened attentively to the computer. He grabbed his computer pad. He had about an hour before the elixir to begin the journey to Mars began to wear off. Geno started to read the computer pad. The ships were being deployed to the Southern Hemisphere. Antarctica was experiencing volcanic activity. Most humans understood the risk of inhabiting Earth Station orbiting Earth and being based on Lunar Base on the Moon, but it was a wild gamble after almost 250 years of space flight and advances in science.

Geno looked at this computer pad again. Kakuro was phoning him. Geno touched the computer pad.

"What happened?" asked Kakuro.

"Ships have been deployed to Earth," answered Geno.

"Why?" asked Kakuro.

"There is seismic and volcanic activity in Antarctica," answered Geno. "Earth Station put a stop to my launch. Hopefully, I don't have a bad metabolic reaction to not being plugged into the ship or go through withdrawals."

"I hope not," said Kakuro.

Only time would tell what would happen to the panic-stricken Geno. Earth was failing the planetary defenses test. It was showing that it was unstable. Geno still didn't understand the reaction of his father Krev to suddenly put him on a spaceship journey. What did Krev want him to do to save Earth? He was only beginning to find out the massive plot the Planetary Defense for Geology and Geography had for Earth. But it somehow involved him.

IV

Geno continued to panic. The elixir was starting to overtake his bodily systems. He started to run through the orbital. He had to get to the Med Orbital. *What is going on?* he thought.

They released too many ships to Earth. Even then, the elixir to help him propel him to Mar should not have backfired with his bodily system. Geno touched his computer pad again. It failed. Kakuro's image did not pop up.

When Geno got to an end to the orbital, he touched another computer pad with his badge. He needed to get into contact with his father. "Where is Krev Ost?" said Geno.

The computer lit up as it began to scan through Earth Station data.

"Krev Ost is located in the Science Orbital," said the Earth Station computer.

Geno blinked. What was he doing? He didn't know there were any scientific experiments occurring. But what was going on? They launched too many spacecraft to Earth. Was Earth breaking up? Beads of sweat started to run down Geno's face. He still needed to make it to the Med Orbital and then make it back to the Launch and Dock Orbital. Would he be able to make it to the Science Orbital to warn his father to launch himself to Mars too?

Everything was moving too quickly. The computer led him into the main part of Earth Station. Geno began to run. Geno wanted someone to be there with him. He held his stomach. He began to puke. He dropped his computer pad on the station's floor. He must make it to the Med Orbital. *Where are Ignacio and Kakuro?* he thought?

Geno continued to run. The elixir continued to backfire, and he began to foam at the mouth.

As Geno was running, he started to develop double and tunnel vision. He could see barely. Geno didn't know how much time had passed or who took his badger, but later he found himself grasping for breath on Med Orbital floor, with artificial intelligence doctors and nurses.

"Is everything all right?" asked one of the AI doctors.

"No," squealed and murmured Geno all at once. "I need a couple of shots to counteract the side effects of the elixir meant for sleep to Mars," ordered Geno.

"All right then," said a group of artificial intelligence nurses and doctors. "But first, we must give you a scan of your body."

"Okay. But hurry," said Geno.

Geno was immediately placed on a medicine table. The body scan started. It scanned for about a minute before the AI doctors and nurses all yelled simultaneously, "Clear!"

"Now we are administering the serum to counteract the elixir meant for sleep to Mars," said one of the AI doctors.

Once the doctors and nurses administered the serum, Geno began immediately to wonder where his father was. He wondered how long does he have until the serum fully kicks in. Geno lost his original computer pad so instead jumped down from the medicine table and began searching the Med Orbital for a computer pad. He was being a bad patient. And he found a computer.

He spoke into the pad. "Please locate Krev Ost."

"He is located in the Science Orbital on level 3," said the computer.

Why hasn't he taken notice that over a dozen spacecraft have already been launched to Earth? What is he trying to do? he thought.

Geno needed to know if his father was performing an experiment and if he knew some of the elixirs backfired on him.

V

Geno emerged from the Med Orbital. He went on to search for his father. The serum was still coursing through his system and his bloodstream. The Science Orbital was on the other side of Earth Station. He was stumbling through the halls of the station until he arrived at the Science Orbital. Some personnel were still monitoring the data received from Earth, and some were evacuated to Launch and Dock Orbitals. Geno looked at his clothes. It still said his last name of Ost. He was trying to see he could identify the other personnel at their monitoring stations as they frantically tried to adjust the geoscience occurring on Earth from Earth Station. Finally, Geno made his way to a lonely monitoring station away from the evacuations and monitoring stations.

He found someone hunched over a monitoring station. Geno touched the person. And when the person looked up, it was his father Krev.

"Geno," he said, "how did you make it here?"

Geno was reluctant to tell him about his experience at the Med Orbital. But he could tell his dad need the serum to counteract the elixir, which prepares people for Mars. Why was it not working for some of the evacuees and presumably letting some die? His father was in pain. So Geno injected a shot he stole from one of the AI doctors and nurses. Krev let out a groan.

"Are you all right, Dad," asked Geno in a frantic voice. "Are you all right?"

"Yes, I am, thanks for the shot," said his father.

His father's pain was subsiding from taking the elixir. His father's hands were still clutched together as if he were protecting something. Were there microchips with hidden information? Geno couldn't tell, but he would know soon.

"Geno," said Krev, "I think someone is trying to sabotage the Planetary Defense for Geology and Geography, but the signals we were detecting to see if it was friend or foe were to out there in space. We must make it Mars Base and from there, Jupiter and Saturn Base. The admiral did not know what was going on when Earth sent out a distress signal. He launched a fleet of spacecraft to assist with the necessary geologic healing process on Earth to all seismic spots on Earth."

Geno started to wonder what his father was saying. What did he mean the admiral did not know what was going on when he launched the spacecraft? Was he still alive? Geno looked at a map of Earth from the monitoring station while his father was recovering from the shot. There was a picture of a major metropolis in the Northern Hemisphere being pummeled by rare volcanic activity not seen since the foundation of the Planetary Defense for Geology and Geography. Geno still wanted to know more from his father, but Earth Station was beginning to lack personnel to keep itself in orbit around Earth. It was only a matter of time before it would put its orbit to decay and disintegrate in Earth's atmosphere. Geno grabbed his father by the arm.

"Dad, let's go," said Geno.

"Hold on! I have something to give you," said Krev.

Geno looked at his father. He did not look well. What was he trying to say? Is he going to make it to the nearest Launch Orbital?

"Try to open my hands," said Geno. Geno could not believe his dad could be dying. But why? Geno was not filled with anger because he knew his dad always give it his all in his endeavors with the Planetary Defense for Geology and Geography and all his doings on Earth Station. Geno opened his father's hands. Within them were some microchips, which Geno had not seen since induction in classified photos. What was his father going to say?

"I believe, and the rest of the crew I have encountered," said Krev, "that it was some kind sabotage effort on Earth and Earth Station. Mars and Lunar Base were not responding, or we were cut off from them once we received a signal from the outer limits of the solar system," he said. "Keep the microchips in your badge."

Geno could not believe that there was a sabotage effort on Earth and the planetary defense. But from where and by who? The eyes of Geno's father began to roll in the back of his head. He was clearly passing. Geno never knew his father's true mission and what it was to rectify the situation on Earth. Millions of people have already died just from this one incident. Geno looked around. He said to himself, "I must make it back to a Launch Orbital for the journey to Mars Base."

Geno started to run to the nearest Launch Orbital. Geno knew that his dad was already dead. There was nothing he could do to save him. He gave him the shot to counteract the elixir he had taken. Geno knew his father would want him to evacuate and live. Geno could feel Earth Station orbit disintegrating. Geno strapped himself into the spaceship and inserted the coordinates to Mars Base.

The spaceship was launched from Mars Base, and an ion sphere began to develop around the ship. It glowed against the solar winds of the sun. Geno darkened the view screen and prepared for ionic sleep. Sooner or later, he knew he would be back to Earth's orbit and find out what happened to Earth and Earth Station and Ignacio. His last thoughts were of his father and his intent to save what remained of the plot of the Planetary Defense for Geology and Geography to rescue Earth from geologic demise.

When Geno woke up, the spaceship was already orbiting Mars. Geno looked around himself. Some foam oozed from his mouth from some of the good elixir given to him by the AI robots back on Earth Station. The situation was growing more complicated by the moment. The elixir was part of intrasellar travel ever since the geologic cataclysm on Earth. It felt like it was losing its potency or something.

Geno knew how conceited humans had become throughout the solar system about the newfound gift of intrasellar and their denial of what was happening back home on the home world. Humans knew this all the way to the Oort Cloud, but shortly before the disintegration of Earth Station orbit around Earth and the blackout of communication, Geno had been wondering what was happening to all the humans based throughout the Oort Cloud. Those bases were a plot for interstellar travel past the solar system.

Suddenly, an image of Kakuro popped up on the view screen. Kakuro did not know at all the preceding events that led to Geno's arrival around Mars. Kakuro looked like Ignacio before the disastrous events.

"Hey," he said, "something weird last night. I tried to take one of those fun trips to the asteroid belt with the elixir, but instead, I woke up around orbiting Mars."

Geno knew that Kakuro was starting to suffer from some of the symptoms.

"I had a dream," said Kakuro.

"What was it?" asked Geno.

Kakuro started to sweat. He described his dream to Geno. It was a dream of a porcupine fish being thrashed by a shark from the earth through the oceans of Europa, the moon that surrounds Jupiter. Geno was perplexed. He did not understand its meaning. Geno was more concerned about the elixir, which was the key to interstellar travel throughout the solar system, and why he was sweating. Did Kakuro even know what was going on with the elixir? As Geno watched more beads of sweat drip down Kakuro's face, was he being sabotaged too? Geno did not know what was occurring on Mars Base; everything seemed stable with known spacecraft leaving the base. He was more concerned with his friend.

VII

Geno was still aboard the spaceship from Earth Station when it started to enter into a disintegrating orbit. Geno felt so sorry for Kakuro. All his childhood memories of him flashed before Geno. Kakuro continued to sweat.

"Oh my god," he said. "I think I'm going to die."

"Hold on," said Geno. "I'm trying to pull the ship out of a decaying orbit."

He inserted coordinates to the poles of Mars for a different orbit than an equatorial one. He knew somehow he had to save Kakuro and Ignacio. His father was already dead, and by now, Earth Station has disintegrated in the atmosphere of Earth. The entire plot to save Earth by the Planetary Defense for Geology and Geography was being sabotaged. But by who? Geno was already at Mars. Did the outer bands of humans who had started a diaspora into space know what had happened to Earth, the Moon, and now Mars?

"Kakuro, how do you feel?" asked Geno.

"I feel horrible," said Kakuro as he gasped for breath.

"Let me send a new chemical equation to recalibrate the serum in you to something livable."

Geno crossed his fingers. Geno touched the nearest computer pad and sent a more intense communication pulse to Kakuro to make sure the chemical equation made it through all the noise of the universe and the solar system.

"Received," said Geno's computer on the spaceship.

Kakuro's signal started to break apart, but his gasping slowed. By this time, Geno's spaceship was firmly in place in a stable orbit around Mars. But what about the sabotage he was experiencing? He was unable to save Ignacio, but Ignacio must have sought shelter somewhere on the dark side of the Moon. Geno prayed that Ignacio's serum in his body did not backfire too, which keeps the journey from Earth to Moon and back short as well. Geno waited for a response from Kakuro. Was Kakuro alive?

Geno's spaceship was orbiting fast like it was about to do a slingshot from Mars to the outer parts of the solar system. The computer started and began to alert Geno. Geno continued to send out a communication pulse from his spaceship. Kakuro did not respond. Instead, the Mars Medical Base did. Images were passing fast on his viewscreen from on his spaceship. It seemed like Mars Base was thrown into chaos. Why? The elixir had completely backfired on almost everyone that keeps them from returning to Earth after the long journey. Geno became frantic and searched for the microchips his father gave him. He must make it to Jupiter Station now that all these images of a chaotic Mars Base were coming across his view screen.

What happened to Kakuro? Geno requested a planetary search for Kakuro. They also carried badges, and the serum could be detected from any spaceship. The computer confirmed Kakuro was a casualty in the mayhem on Mars. Geno started to cry.

I must make it to Jupiter, thought Geno.

The moons around them still had data that would inform him what was happening to Earth and why sabotage was starting and why so many of his friends were dead or presumed dead. There were so many questions. Were the outer-limit humans of the solar ship solar system still alive? As Geno's spaceship continued to accelerate in its orbit around Mars, he started to cry. He was beginning to feel he was also being sabotaged. Geno was starting to give up. As he was beginning to pass out, he sent out one last communication. This time it was solar system-wide.

VIII

Geno was attempting to wake up from a lucid dream of extraterrestrial animals he had only heard and seen on coded microchips or rumors on the Earth Station and conversations with Ignacio. He kept trying to open his eyes. And every time, he became unconscious but still breathing. Geno was still aboard the spacecraft, and he somehow managed to touch a medical kit with an oxygen patch he could use to help him breathe.

A couple of hours later, he woke up to find himself docked at Jupiter Station. It was eerily quiet on board his ship. When Geno opened his eyes, it appeared his pilot and computer console had been scrambled. A hissing sound was emitting from his communication device. He looked to his left and began to turn himself away from the cramped quarters of his ship because he noticed that the ship was fully docked. He had one procedure: It was to open the doorway to Jupiter Station. And he did so. Geno stood straight up in the tunnel extending from Jupiter Station. His legs were wobbling from the sudden jettison from Mars orbit and maneuvering past the asteroid belt. He tried not to think about the loss of life he had personally experienced, also the loss of life on Earth. Geno never had felt lonely in his life.

He touched his communication badge. He tried to contact Ignacio, but all it did was emit the same hissing sound and a bit of static. Geno knew what was on Jupiter Station. He had the microchips from Lunar Base, the information from Mars, and his own knowledge and training. He needed to find out if anyone was on Jupiter Station. He touched his thumb to a doorway key. When the doorway opened, it was as eerily quiet as it was on his ship. He started to walk down a hallway and came upon a console with emergency lighting. He glanced at it, but a video recording had been interrupted by some kind of intense magnetic pulse through the station. He must make it to the deck of the chief science officer. There, he will find his answer.

Until then, Geno had an ion gun in case there was an intruder from a faction on Earth. As Geno held up his gun and put both hands around it, he grew nervous. Was Jupiter Station where the trouble started? The people here were supposed to help send data and recalibrate the geologic planetary defense system to help heal Earth for the time being. Geno only went too far with the planetary defense for geology. He had heard the Jupiter Station was preparing for evacuees from Earth, but why did Earth lose its geologic stability so suddenly? In truth, it became hard for humans to understand the gravity of the situation Earth was in, but they did the best they could.

Geno finally made it to the deck of the chief science officer. The deck was big and expansive. There was a seeing screen with a holographic image of Mars and Earth spinning on either side of the screen. For some reason, all communication and operational data stopped transmitting to Jupiter Station. Geno came closer to all the consoles, where officers, civilians, and cadets should have been maintaining their stations. Geno began to sweat. He wanted to talk to anyone. Was anyone out there? Geno finally came to one console, and there was a communication badge that had the ability to activate at the console. He pressed the badge against the console to activate it. The sounds that came through the badge were only of horrific screams. Geno had hoped the people of Jupiter Station had evacuated or made friendly contact with whatever or whoever was out there in the solar system and beyond. His hopes were dashed incredibly.

Whoever or whatever the foe may be, was it some kind of predator? Are sentient species, which he had made contact with, capable of interstellar travel? There was one plausibility, however remote: There could still be humans tricking Geno into believing all this. A fraction after the emptiness of Jupiter station. Geno gulped. He knew what a human would be after the final secret of humanity to save who was left on Earth. Geno looked at a console and inserted two of the five microchips given to him by his father. He knew what he was about to violate. He did not want to look down at what the console was to reveal but instead moved his fingers to activate the seeing screen. And there it was on the seeing screen: the interstellar ship. Geno was analyzing the schematic hidden behind one of Jupiter's moons. So they were not humans after Geno or Earth. Whoever started the sabotage of the planetary defense system had to be from beyond the solar system.

Geno immediately put his badge on the console and let a retinal scan give him access to the interstellar ship. The only way to get to the new ship was through the ship he arrived on when he got to Jupiter Station. He knew of what lay beyond Jupiter, rumors of fantastic creatures from another realm, solar system or galaxy, or whatever. Geno immediately removed his badge from the console and ended the retinal scan. He quickly ran through every doorway and hallway that was opened by the retinal scan and found his way back to the ship. Geno's ship responded adequately and inputted the final coordinates to the interstellar ship located behind one of Jupiter's moons.

IX

Geno reached the interstellar ship called *Joxer*. It was massive compared to Jupiter Station. He got on board and activated the emergency protocol, and one chair emerged from the center for lone human to navigate to safety and perhaps fire a couple of ion weapons before being boarded and taken hostage.

He sat in the chair, but he started to feel dizzy. He was more than feeling the effects of space. And he wished Ignacio was here. He tapped his communication by his ear to see if he was still out there. Something was coming in, but it did not sound like Ignacio, and it was coded. Geno took an elixir pill to ease the side effects of his space travels and the interstellar travel to come. Geno looked straight forward to the seeing screen and inputted coordinates to Saturn. Before he left the orbit of one of Jupiter's moons, he received a communication from Ignacio. It was a visual image and not a verbal message. Geno also knew Ignacio had a quirky sense of humor, but the image that popped up on the seeing screen beguiled Geno. It was simply a picture of ancient human 7-Up soda can spinning on its side against the backdrop of the darkness of space. Geno thought of what it could mean. Ignacio was always a fan of human history before the great cataclysm.

The image was the start of some kind of visual rhyme game which Ignacio did not have time to complete. Geno took the image of the seeing screen and inputted coordinates to Saturn and prepared for more interstellar travel. It would take about an hour of Earth time to get to Saturn. Geno needed to take some rest so he decided to take a sleeping pill.

When Geno woke up, he found himself orbiting Saturn above its rings. They were beautiful according to a human this far in the future from what humans initially took them as ugly in the past. The rings were perfectly aligned. Geno wanted and started to get up from the chair in the center of the deck, but something out of the corner of his eye distracted him. It was a beam of light jumping around the deck behind him. Geno was no linguist or extraterrestrial zoologist or anthropologist or anyone of that nature. But the beam of light seemed to be communicating. Geno turned around, but by that time, the beam of light jumped into the computer console. Geno knew that back on Earth, these types of phenomena are called tricks of the eye, but this time the beam of light affected a code of the console and throughout the ship. Humans before him had called these phenomena "sprites" this far out in the solar system.

Geno activated his badge and communication device to record this interaction. The seeing screen was suddenly activated, and an innocent image of Earth's Moon silently rotating popped up in the middle of the screen. Geno thought of Ignacio, but as soon as he did, a horrific image of Earth came to pass. The sky was full of plumes of darkened ash and smoke. On some continents, lakes of glowing lava were seen, and the oceans had turn brown on the coast and the tropics. Geno looked to see what date it was to predict this final cataclysm of Earth.

Geno just shook his head. Suddenly, the sprite phenomenon jumped out of the console and wrapped around his finger. The tingling sensation suggested to place his finger on the navigation bar, and he did. The navigation information released was a route to the planet Uranus. Geno couldn't conceive why; he grew frightened. He would lose contact with Ignacio and whoever was left on Lunar Base. The sprite was not giving up. As soon as Geno resisted swiping his finger to coincide with his cognitive thought process to navigate, the ship moved slowly away from Saturn's rings, and suddenly, he was propelled to the middle distance between Saturn and Uranus.

X

When Geno was at the middle distance between Saturn and Uranus, the interstellar ship called *Joxer* began to twirl against the gravity of Uranus. The sprite jumped out of the console and jumped straight into the seeing screen and presumably out into the void. All that was left on the console before Geno was a quote from a poem of Edgar Allen Poe, and it read, "Is *all* that we see or seem but a dream within a dream."

Geno composed himself. His psyche was disturbed by this message; perhaps it was the sleeping pills he had been taking. He didn't want to know, out here in the vast outreaches of the solar system, that everything was a dream, whether it was a joke or trick from Ignacio or some clever extraterrestrial or some other life form.

Suddenly, from the seeing screen appeared a form ready to enchant Geno. Geno balked away from the form, but as soon as he did so, it began to glow a golden yellow. Geno tried to understand what was going on at first through Ignacio's now lame message in human history called "tripping out," but his medical analysis said he was not hallucinating and the entity could communicate.

"Well, hello," said the humanoid form. "My name is Oberon," he said in a deep, assertive voice.

"And what do you want?" asked Geno.

"Want? That is not a concept I understand. But you human species are on the brink of collapse throughout the solar system, and if my kind don't render aid quick enough, perhaps humans may go extinct," said the humanoid form Oberon.

Geno found his words to him curt and unwelcoming, but Geno touched his communication badge, and the translation came across much better. Geno furrowed his brow. He was trained in first-contact procedures, but for some reason, this humanoid form seemed a bit inept from the data collected about how strong and mighty extraterrestrial and other space life forms should look like.

"Do you need assistance?" asked Geno.

"Yes, I do," said Oberon. "It seems that our two species have been caught in a fight of sorts. Your planet called Earth is in grave peril as is the existence of my species."

"But why?" asked Geno.

"Well, there's a catch if I tell you anything further," said Oberon.

And as soon as he completed his statement, the sprite jumped back into the ship and went into the weapon systems of *Joxer*, the interstellar ship. Geno did not like the fact that the phenomena were trying to arm the ship even further. Geno tried to block the inputs of the sprite but failed.

"Do we need to be armed?" he addressed Oberon.

"Well, yes, we do need to be armed," replied Oberon.

"But why? I'm not understanding. I was only on a mission to find out why Earth's geologic defense systems had been sabotaged either by humans or non-humans and hope for message and collaboration of peace," said Geno.

"Spoken almost like a true diplomat," said Oberon. "Perhaps that's why this happens to you, but we're not that species who is concerned with fate and politics."

"Then what are you concerned about?" asked Geno.

"Concern of humans rarely irritated our kind," answered Oberon. "However, to keep this trade with humans before you embark on your interstellar journey, we, unfortunately, miscalculated how soon and quick Earth would become unstable."

"Then what are the rest of the humans to do if you are claiming you miscalculated some kind of geologic and cosmologic effect on Earth?" asked Geno.

Oberon sighed. "Well, the phenomena you call a sprite, its actual name is Puck, a helper of the sort where I am from," answered Oberon. "Yes, and the real secret between you and our species, we are caught in a fight."

"Well, if it's a fight you're looking for, humanity is not really prepared," said Geno.

"Ah, and never were my kind prepared for a fight," said Oberon. "We developed a weapon system quickly, but it was almost too late until we decided to sabotage Earth Station and all the rest of the stations."

"You did WHAT!?" screamed Geno.

"The typical response that my people were expecting from you, Geno," said Oberon. "But still, there is a far greater foe than I. That foe bargained a bit too high."

"Then where is he or she?" Geno asked, fuming. "Geological stability on Earth was not the result of sabotage, I know, but what happened to the stations are!"

Geno looked at what the sprite named Puck was doing to the navigation console. It was inputting navigation coordinates past the solar system a bit and into what is known as the Oort Cloud. Geno had only heard faint rumors of humans traveling to that region of space.

XI

Geno slowly conceded to the life form named Puck. He had the navigation console now. The humanoid form of Oberon was still on the main deck of the spaceship *Joxer*. Its next destination seemed to be the Oort Cloud. However, the spaceship *Joxer* was clearly not ready for the space environment being thrown at it. *What was in the Oort Cloud?* wondered Geno. *Oberon seemed unconcerned and more concerned that we reach the edge of the Oort Cloud. How can being all the way out here in the solar system help save Earth and the stations?*

At first, Geno's task on Mars was scary, but he thought it would be simple to recalibrate the planetary geologic defense system to give Earth more time.

Geno looked over at Oberon. Oberon seemed to be in a mental state as if he was reading Geno's mind. Oberon winked.

"Yes, you're right about your concern, Geno," Oberon said. "What are we doing out here is a good question. Needless to say the enemy, which my kind— our kind—are concerned about, have vested interested with being out here."

"Well, what happened to the people of Jupiter Station?" asked Geno.

"Well, they met their demise," answered Oberon, "with clemency, might I add, as to what end they should face."

"But did the enemy choose the demise of so many people aboard Jupiter Station?" said Geno.

"In the words of this enemy of yours and mine, the history has been reached. Even then, this has been a hard bargain because their end did not justify the historicalness of all this. Humans haven't met a fate in battle in quite some time," said Oberon.

Oberon snapped his fingers, and the sprite Puck quickly came to his side. Geno stood beside the solitary chair on the deck and looked at the seeing screen as if he were ready for a retinal scan. Instead, Geno's surroundings disappeared.

Oberon and Puck were still there, but from the looks of his surroundings, Geno found himself on different astral plane of existence. Oberon sighed again about Geno. A form or a friendly sprite did not form in from of Geno or to his side. But a voice as foreign as some of the ancient languages began to articulate Geno's name. Geno's communication device and hearing device disappeared.

Geno's sense of duality was at stake. Oberon had the sprite Puck ward off the plummeting feeling of depression often experienced by humans. Geno touched his badge one last time in hopes that Ignacio was still alive, and a beep sounded. Ignacio, luckily, was still alive.

Oberon remained silent, and Puck remained still, only glimmering against the faint change of color of this different astral plane of existence. Geno kept staying at the faint change of color of the astral plane.

"And what do the three of you want?" asked a voice.

Geno was surprised the entity was even revering to the sprite Puck. Oberon quickly took charge. "We've come not to be just diplomats, Juno, but in human terms, this time a bargain must be struck. You have the power to save humankind and mine," said Oberon.

"Does human knowledge understand what I am and what I am capable of doing?" asked Juno.

"He doesn't," said Oberon.

"What do you mean I don't know or understand this entity is capable of doing?" retorted Geno.

"It's always been a ruse," said Juno.

"A ruse," said Geno, "but why? My people are honest and forthright and have subdued insurmountable obstacles to the future of my species."

"But I still want to destroy you and your kind," said Juno. "Your kind have proved unworthy of the duality which you experienced between Oberon and yourself."

"What do you mean?" said Geno, almost hysterical.

"In human speak, and not to insult your intelligence, Geno, what would the four entities here require to destroy at least?" said Juno. "And mind you, I am not very philosophical."

"I still don't know what you mean," answered Geno.

Oberon remained distant from Geno's side, and so did Puck.

"Maybe I need to make myself more obvious," said Juno. "I've been watching. But I am only an entity bound almost by the same cosmological forces as humans may be one day. But you proved something through action for one thing."

"Then don't destroy Earth or any human if we proved worthy and I," said Geno.

"Ah, getting close who you disturbed human being," said Juno. "Remember all is a dream but within a dream."

"Well, yes, I remember," said Geno.

"Well, you're referring to my friend, one of my last friends after this tragedy," said Juno.

"They were right," said Juno in a fading voice, and then suddenly, Geno was hit with a pulsating beam of light and landed on the deck of *Joxer*, the spaceship.

XII

Geno woke up to Ignacio on Lunar Base.

"Oh my god, what happened?" said Ignacio. "The Earth's core is becoming unstable."

Geno looked around. He still had all his badges and devices. A beeping sound emitted from his body, and he started to fumble around his suit for the microchips given by his father. Geno had a throbbing headache.

"Here, take these microchips," said Geno. "Just take them and input them into the global defense system and computer."

"Are you certain there are only a few humans left on Lunar Base?" asked Ignacio.

"Yes. Do it," answered Geno.

Despite the fact that Geno and Ignacio had just been inducted into the planetary defense for geology, Ignacio obeyed Geno's orders. Suddenly, Earth's geologic stability alert system went to stage 2. But the damage had already been done to the Earth's climate and geology. Evacuations were proceeding as planned.

"You saved countless lives," said Ignacio. "How did you do it?"

"Thanks, but no, thanks," said Geno about repeating the story.

"Do you know how you got here?" asked Ignacio.

Geno smirked. *I got here only through a fairy tale.* "What's going on on Earth?" asked Geno.

"Earth's geology and climate are still unstable!" shouted Ignacio, going to another console.

Geno felt like puking. He got up from the floor and made his way to the nearest private quarters onboard Lunar Base. Over a sink, Geno splashed some water to his face and patted the back of his sweaty neck with a towel. After he finished drying his face, Geno patted around his suit for one last microchip.

"Forgetting something?" asked a voice Geno barely recognized.

Geno whipped around and saw Oberon and the sprite Puck.

Oberon grabbed Geno's arm and opened his fist. In it is the key to Earth's future and the future of humanity. "But what is it?" asked Geno. "I'm just glad to see my friend before we evacuated."

"Well, hurry along and give it to Ignacio," said Oberon.

"Yes, sir," said Geno.

Geno ran through all the corridors and finally came across Ignacio and some civilians and a cadet. Who would understand him? Is it too late? "Here," Geno said to Ignacio. "Input this schematic to save Earth. It's just not any other microchip."

The cadet gave him a weary-eyed look. The civilian quickly left the room, noticing that this had nothing to do with evacuation. Ignacio grabbed the microchip.

"Well, will this save Earth?" asked Ignacio.

"Something close to it," Geno quipped.

Ignacio inputted it, and it showed a schematic of some kind of sphere—a couple of centuries before the establishment of the planetary defense of geology referred to as Dyson sphere. Some of the technology in the year 2350 resembled it, but the microchip went beyond a schematic to save Earth.

Ignacio was elated. "This has the potential to override the planetary defense geologic grid for the best, including Earth's and Mars's," he said. The planetary defense geologic grid now had enough power to subdue and change the geologic forces affecting Earth.

Geno went to the docking bay area to return to Earth. He had enough of this space journey and potentially saving humanity; it just was not in his credentials. In the shuttle bay dock, Geno heard a knock. Ignacio was there. "Geno, I think you are forgetting something. I don't know what it is, but it's one of those century-old things I'm fascinated by," said Ignacio.

Geno grabbed the item from his hand and nodded. And Ignacio quickly went back out through the other dock door. Geno opened his hand. It was a Chinese fortune cookie. Geno broke it in half. And it read, "Is *all* that we see or seem but a dream within a dream?"

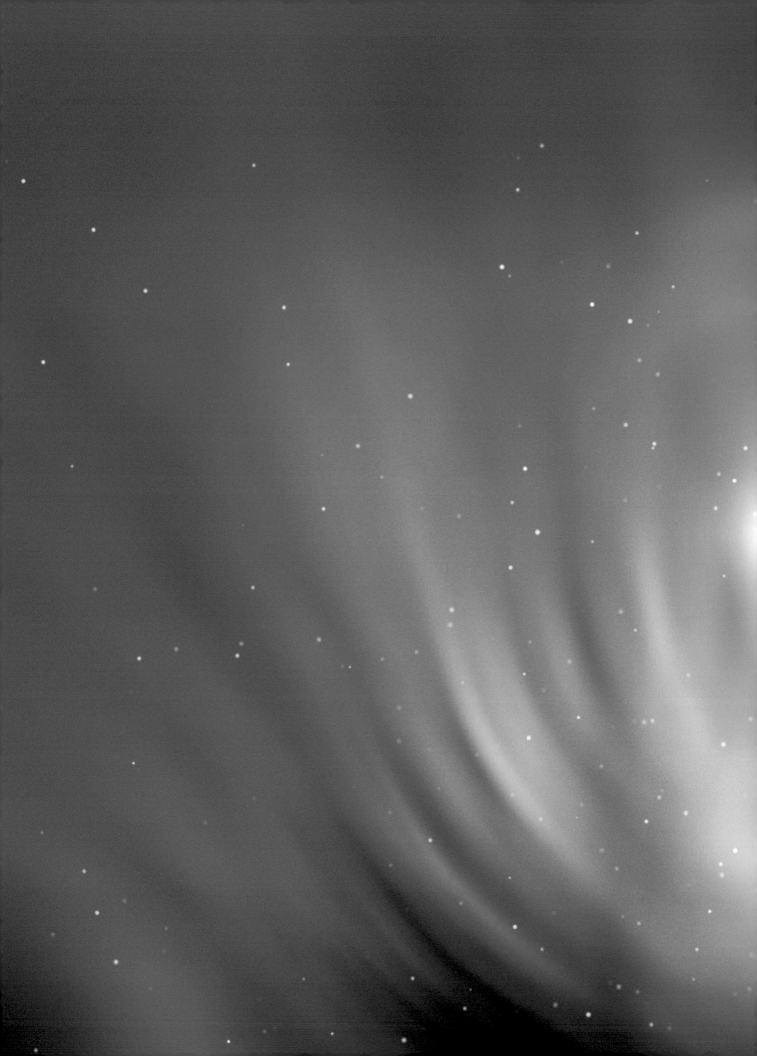

Printed in the United States
by Baker & Taylor Publisher Services